MANTIS SQUAD

GORDON BOSTIC

ISBN (Paperback): 979-8-218-28201-1
ISBN (E-book): 979-8-218-28202-8

Printed in the United States of America

Dedication

*To my sister, Becky, for her love,
support and encouragement.*

Contents

Once in a Million Births

Maybe once in a million births
A special child is born
Who is blessed with abilities
That most would view with scorn.

Their parents noticed diff'rences
The moment they were born.
Where some tiny indications
Were clearly meant to warn.

Though love had never been denied
Some caution was maintained.
For there were aspects each had shown
That could not be explained.

Their children's gifts their parents hid
Because they were afraid
Of what the government may do
Should their secrets be made.

The Grand Experiment

It was a grand experiment
The major had proposed.
Her subjects had been targeted
Which some on high opposed.

They weren't exactly volunteers
But all were dangerous.
At some point they must deal with them
Which had been obvious.

One day they may become a threat
So, this had been her plan
To bring them in to work for her
And train the best they can.

The hierarchy saw nothing wrong
With seeing the plan through.
It's nothing more than conscription
Which governments can do.

Her goal to train an elite squad
Who had abilities
The government could call upon
Whenever it should please.

A squad to do the dirty work
That no one wished to do
Or to handle situations
No law was written to.

Trained to be a praying mantis
Who would seduce their prey.
Then given opportunity
Their victim coldly slay.

A Nobody

Most thought he was a nobody
So, none had paid him heed.
He was not known to socialize
As he'd not seen the need.

He had greater aspirations
Than any could have known.
While they had found initiative
Something he'd never shown.

The man a total mystery
That no one wished resolved.
For none in truth had a desire
To with him be involved.

They believed that he was stagnant
Who had no chance to grow.
As a man with no ambition
He had no place to go.

The Raids

It's clear they'd all been scrutinized
Since they were very young.
As each of them was targeted
Until the trap was sprung.

It was the middle of the night
When for them they had come.
For the government was hopeful
Of what they could become.

The intruders were dressed in black
With no emblems displayed
And refused to identify
The reasons for the raid.

Their parents weren't allowed to know
What was to come of them.
They were direct and to the point
Though questions would condemn.

With each escorted from their home
And sedative was fed.
Which provided the illusion
Each one of them was dead.

The government had taken them
As though they'd no free will.
Because it found it coveted
Their talent or their skill.

The Facility

They woke to find they're prisoners
In some facility.
It was a very sterile place
That lacked frivolity.

They herded each into a room
As they were each brought in.
Not one had dared to speak a word
Though guards would flash a grin.

As they stared at one another
Their questions were the same.
What entity had brought them here
And reason it would claim.

The room was very dimly lit
As though it's meant to hide
The ones it held as prisoners
Who had been locked inside.

Their fear was clearly evident
As that their eyes revealed.
Though Skye did not need ESP
To see what they concealed.

The oldest of them was nineteen
And said her name was Skye.
They chose her as their spokeswoman
Though she had not known why.

Skye asked the guards who was in charge
As to them she would speak.
She told them not to lie to her
As that would anger pique.

One guard said to mind her manners
They'd get to them in time.
He had guessed that she was diff'rent
Which to him was a crime.

As they sat in abject silence
And at each other stared.
Not to know what they'd in common
That forced them to be paired.

The Ruling Class

It believed it was pragmatic
Children taken and trained
To carry out the objectives
That it had entertained.

For only it had known the truth
Which served the greater good.
The populace was ignorant
Thus, had not understood.

The populace were merely sheep
Who needed to be led.
For they'd believed in foolishness
As that was what they're fed.

They believed in equality
Which was a made-up lie.
It's destined as the ruling class
To whom rules don't apply.

With unbounded aspirations,
It was a juggernaut.
Beyond the reach of lawfulness
No chance it could be caught.

So, it believed it's justified
In any choice it made.
And there's no one to intercede,
Thus, it was unafraid.

Major Miller

Major Miller was a hard ass
Who made it very clear
He had need of their services
Thus, why they were brought here.

Their lives he had claimed ownership
Where they were to be trained
To undertake special missions
The government ordained.

Their training would be rigorous
And failure not allowed.
They'd do what was required of them
Or privilege disallowed.

Then Skye stood up and yelled at him
That this had not been fair.
Skye read that he was furious
But truly did not care.

Miller motioned guards to take her
And Skye was led away.
As the others watched in silence
Where they'd nothing to say.

Introductions

Miller called for introductions
Then proved that he had known
The secrets that their parents kept
And talents they had shown.

Here their names were unimportant
Though first names they'd retain.
They'd no need for identities
For what they were to train.

Skye was the one they led away
Whose secret specialty
Was she was highly perceptive
Due to her ESP.

Jade was clearly oriental
Who's agile to a fault.
A gymnastic phenomenon
The way she'd leap and vault.

Brie had a special quality
That was hard to define.
Men found her irresistible
And for her men would pine.

Chris was ultra-acrobatic
And seemed to have no bones.
She, too, was a contortionist
Like no other they'd known.

Lynn was an illusionist who
Could make any believe
Whatever she had wished them to
From what she could conceive.

Though Jill possessed a high IQ
That measured off the chart,
Miller felt it had been tempered
Because she had a heart.

Kat was closer to her namesake
Than many would believe.
As her vision and her hearing
Only cats could achieve.

The government had chosen them
For their abilities.
For each of them were so unique
In capabilities.

None of them were super-human
Nor mutants or the like.
But each with an ability
That in them seemed to spike.

The Ground Rules

They knew the woman was a bitch
The moment she walked in.
For she had been condescending
And sly had been her grin.

She addressed them in a manner
That had made their skin crawl.
She seemed cold and calculating
As though above them all.

Born with innate abilities,
Each one of them a prize
And why each had been selected
For this bold enterprise.

It was a team they would become
With code name Mantis Squad.
That's meant to serve the government
And be its hand of God.

For just like a praying mantis
Who once they choose a mate
Takes assessment of their partner
To then decapitate.

And just like a praying mantis
They would not hesitate
In a quick determination
What was their victim's fate.

They found that collars had been placed
Around each of their throat.
The bitch had said for discipline
Then showed them the remote.

She pushed a button as she smiled
To see their agony.
The collars were electrical
And shocks, reality.

The pain nearly unbearable
Reduced them all to tears.
While the bitch said it's a warning
Should training find arrears.

Then the bitch had set the ground rules
Under which they would train.
Where any failures would be met
With this mind searing pain.

Blank told them that they had no worth
Beyond what they're assigned.
And this would be their destiny
To which they were resigned.

The guards then led them all away
With training to begin.
Where they all had felt so helpless
In the state they were in.

Brie asked her guard who was the bitch.
He replied Doctor Blank.
She would oversee their training
And she loved to pull rank.

Doctor Blank

Doctor Blank a contradiction
Who had a troubled soul.
She had no faith in anything
That she did not control.

This project was the only thing
She'd thought about for years.
And the prospect of its failure
One of her greatest fears.

Though she knew the guards disliked her
She had not really cared.
As they were simply implements
For one who greatly dared.

She swore she would do anything
To see the project through.
If anyone should threaten that
She feared what she may do,

For her career was on the line
With how the project ends.
So, she'd no time for niceties
Or any use for friends.

Brie

When first arrived, they hated Brie
As she had favors shown.
The others only knew abuse
With no favors known.

Brie was not truly beautiful
But she had an allure.
That had seemed to draw Men to her
As though she was a lure.

The guards were always kind to her
As sultry was her way.
She'd teased it may be possible
They'd be with her one day.

Though Brie had done nothing special.
It simply was her way.
She knew men would respond to her
As to her men were clay.

She had never understood it
But gift she had received.
For men were putty in her hand
To do as she believed.

The Dormitory

The dormitory that they shared
Had allowed interplay.
Though they were not all that cordial
When first they came to stay.

At first there was a lack of trust
As they were strangers all.
Their only commonality
That to this fate they'd fall.

The room itself was truly stark
With seven trunks and beds.
There was a bathroom to be shared
With seven shower heads.

They sat in silence as they stared
At each one in the room.
Each with a sense of loneliness
Mixed with a sense of doom.

It was Jill who broke the silence
To say they should agree
Whatever now was happening
They were not going free.

She felt there's none that they could trust
Who lived outside their room.
For now they all should play along
Because of threats that loom.

Then as she fingered her collar
The others clearly saw
She feared they may be monitored
Which brought the others awe.

Jade

She seemed to be a normal girl
Until that fateful day.
When circumstances had arose
Where she'd not walked away.

It happened quite by accident
Her secret had been freed.
Where there had been an accident
When caution she'd not heed.

A building façade broke away
Where someone had been trapped.
Jade freed the man from the debris
While those who watched had clapped.

It was nothing that she worked at
But had come naturally.
She almost looked too feminine
For this reality.

That event changed friends' perceptions
Where few to her would speak.
For most became afraid of her
Believing her a freak.

Blank's Concerns

When Peter spoke to Doctor Blank
And said this was not fair.
Doctor Blank simply stared at him
And wondered why he'd care.

Bank thought mistakes may have been made
With the guards strictly male.
Where some feelings may develop
To cause this all to fail.

Although now they were committed
With project underway.
There could be no further changes
As all were here to stay.

So, Blank went to Major Miller
To speak of her concern.
The Major said he'd handle it
Though look was more than stern.

The Major issued an edict
That if his guards were wise
The girls would all be left alone
And with none fraternize.

Where any who would disobey
Punishment would be swift.
For any who'd approach the girls
He'd simply set adrift.

Major Miller was a stickler
For orders he received
And Doctor Blank was not in charge
Despite what she believed.

Chris

Chris hated what they took from her
As she had not agreed
To be a tool that Blank would use
Wherever she saw need.

Chris was the youngest of the group
As she was just fifteen.
And lacking in maturity
She was caught in between.

She wished to trust the older girls
But had not known them well.
And now, in this environment
Was just one step from hell.

Chris felt that she was all alone
And missed her family.
She'd not seen herself as special
And thus, her quandary.

She had not fully understood
Why she was even here.
The others were much more mature
And had seemed less to fear.

But Chris was not prepared for this
And wanted to go home.
She'd let the others save the world
As tears would freely roam.

At Mess

That night some guards had come for them
As it was dinnertime.
Where they found the mess divided
As though they'd done some crime.

In isolation from the rest
They ate their meal alone.
Where food had been laid out for them
And no selection shown.

There're none who would acknowledge them
As though they were not there.
And no one dared to speak with them
Though some had dared to stare.

So, they ate their meal in silence
Till Jill looked up and said
What the others had been thinking
But chose to leave unsaid.

There was no calvary to come
As they were on their own.
There was no justice due to them
As they were all alone.

Jill told them that they must unite
If they were to survive.
As Blank, she thought, would kill them all
If goal they should deprive.

They saw they were the focal point
Of dinnertime debate.
From the glances and the pointing
There's something they'd berate.

Jill said it would be nice to know
The subject of their talk.
For it had been animated
And some began to gawk.

Kat said their talk had been of them
And they were all afraid.
She heard their whispers and read lips
They thought the special made.

The Party Girl

Though Lynn had been a party girl
Who liked her party ways.
But found in Kat what she desired
So gone were party days.

She'd taken nothing serious
And thought life was a game.
She'd not had a relationship
With any she could name.

She'd no worries of tomorrow
Living just for today.
And shirked responsibilities
As all she did was play.

So, when she had been abducted
The only thing she'd thought
Her party ways caught up to her
And why she had been caught.

But it seemed that her abduction
Had given her new life.
For here was where she first met Kat
Who'd one day be her wife.

The Law Suits

Their parents each had filed a suit
To have their daughters freed.
But judges had been circumspect
As they'd not seen the need.

If government had need of them,
It clearly could recruit.
So, judges had been reluctant
To move forth with each suit

Though they claimed their homes invaded
And daughters were kidnapped.
The judges had been hesitant
For fear they would be trapped.

As agents of the government
They had no wish to rile
Whomever was responsible
For projects of this style.

So, all the suits had been dismissed
For lack of evidence.
Believing parents were too poor
To maintain their offense.

But the bailiff caught Jill's parents
Before they left the court
And said there're other families
Who made the same report.

Then slipped them a piece of paper
Before he disappeared
That had contained a list of names
Where addresses appeared.

Kat

Kat was unsure of who she was
To which most teens attest.
She knew that she was different
But limits would not test.

No boy had ever caught her eye
Nor interest had shown.
And now, she thought, that deep inside
She, somehow, must have known.

She'd heard the snide remarks they made
And though they hurt a lot,
There's no response that she could give
To change their train of thought.

It heightened insecurities
Already she possessed.
As fear of inadequacies
Had left her more depressed.

The truth had only come to her
When she laid eyes on Lynn.
Her heart had nearly skipped a beat
The moment Lynn walked in.

Though she could not quite explain it,
It was love at first sight.
She only hoped Lynn felt the same
Which was her greatest fright.

The Guards

Their guards were hardened veterans
Whose service was their life.
They all seemed like men of honor
But none possessed a wife.

They all had seemed so serious
And most devoid of joy.
They displayed no sense of humor
All, that is, but the boy.

Their guards were all unresponsive
To any question asked.
Their job had been, escort the girls,
Which they did as they're tasked.

But Pete seemed the lone exception
That had not seemed so bad.
In fact, it seemed, he liked the girls
At least, they thought, he had.

Though his valor was unquestioned
He had been pretty young.
By far the youngest of the guards
And not as quite high strung.

Although most the guards had feared them
Peter had not been one.
For he enjoyed their company
And, somehow, Jade's heart won.

Jade Could not Help Herself

Jade could not help but glance at him
Whenever she'd the chance.
Perhaps she only fooled herself
Pete, too, would steal a glance.

Jade found Peter was kind to her
Oblivious to Brie.
As though Brie's charms were lost on him
And Jade all he could see.

Though the rules as Jade had known them
They weren't to fraternize.
But Jade found she could not help herself
Looking into his eyes.

Though she clearly thought him handsome,
He still had been a guard.
And though she found she yearned for him
Danger can't disregard.

Though Skye had thought it very sweet
She also was concerned.
If Jade should be involved with him
Skye feared Jade may get burned.

For Peter had been much older
And probably more wise.
Where Skye feared he'd take advantage
Or Jade may compromise.

A Dark Part of the Government

A dark part of the government
Supported Blank's project.
For it knew of situations
Where change it must effect.

The military had been good
But often left a trail.
Despite its tight security
Was sometimes prone to fail.

It needed anonymity
If goals should be achieved.
For there were threats to be removed
Where blame can't be perceived.

For what it wanted was results
Where none could level blame.
And the Mantis Squad seemed perfect
Despite the stupid name.

The Illusionist

Lynn's teachers were annoyed with her
For use of slight-of-hand.
Where sometimes things would disappear
Or small thing would expand.

Some guards had thought she was a witch
With stunts that she would pull.
There're more than one who were afraid
For she was a handful.

Although they knew it was a trick
That they could not explain.
It still was creepy what she did
Where fear they'd not contain.

They'd heard she's an illusionist
But that could not explain
What they had thought were miracles
Which had been her domain.

They worried what she'd really do
If she was unrestrained.
For now, the collar held in check
The havoc she contained.

The Trainers

The trainers all had been hand picked
And under Blank's command.
Where each were touted specialists
That were in high demand.

Their loyalty to Doctor Blank
Had bordered on insane.
As each directive that she gave
She'd no need to explain.

Her instructions were specific
To which they all were pledged.
With ev'ry girl to be transformed
Where each would be hard-edged.

And the penalty for failure,
Each trainer had been told,
Would be both swift and permanent.
For Blank had been that bold.

A Rise to Leadership

It's Jill who rose to leadership
As in her they believed.
She'd proved so intelligent and
Not easily deceived.

She seemed to be a natural
As though people could sense
Her logic was impeccable
Which she'd gladly dispense..

Jill had exuded confidence
Her choices always right.
That drew from others their belief
She was a guiding light.

That was the story of her life
Though she had not known why.
Where even as a little girl
On her friends would rely.

Perhaps it was her high IQ
That allowed her to see
The solution to a puzzle
With such crisp clarity.

Whenever there was questioning
It's Jill to whom they'd turn.
She always knew just what to say
To lessen their concern.

The Infirmary

Doctor Reed was the head of it
And only one on staff.
His office the infirmary
Serving on their behalf.

And it had been very busy
Since the girls first arrived.
In fact, the doctor was surprised
That any had survived.

He'd dealt mainly with contusions
As true wounds had been rare.
For Blank had a strict policy
The trainers were aware.

While the doctor's job was simple
And was made very plain.
No training sessions to be missed
Despite how great the pain.

Kat and Lynn

Skye saw how Lynn had looked at Kat
Where Kat returned Lynn's glance.
But none considered it a fact
There's a budding romance.

While lack of trust kept most apart
Those two spent time alone.
Yet, no one had seemed curious
To what seeds had been sown.

The fact that they were secretive
Had clearly been a sign.
Though no one else had seemed to see it
Or thought it was benign.

For Kat a new experience
That she'd not known before.
As love had been a mystery
She'd not dared to explore.

Though their love may be forbidden
It had been no less real.
While Kat had found it difficult
To tell Lynn how she'd feel.

Not Freaks of Nature

A team of scientists brought in
Who're to evaluate
The scope of their abilities
And, also, mental state.

They performed tests on each of them
But results were unclear.
Their gifts had seemed to be innate
And that much had been clear.

They were not some freak of nature
Nor something engineered.
They simply had some special gifts
To which they were endeared.

Though only women were allowed
In the study of Brie.
For men Brie could manipulate
And all too easily.

Though when she saw the first reports
Blank seemed to change her mind.
For Blank, it seemed, grew wary of
The things that they may find.

So, scientists she had dismissed
Fearing what they may find.
They begged her not to let them go
But she'd not change her mind.

Their Training

Their training multifaceted
That stretched throughout the day.
Where they had tasks they must perform
In which they had no say.

They all faced training differently
Depending on their skill.
Though all were trained in hand-to-hand
And martial arts to drill.

Their training had been arduous
With little mercy shown.
They weren't allowed to make mistakes
For each one brought a groan.

They needed them to be unfazed
No matter what occurred.
So, they pushed them to their limits
Of what could be endured.

And punishment came swift to those
Who had failed to obey.
Disagreements were not welcomed
To anything they'd say.

They were taught to never question
Directives they received.
They're meant to serve the greater good
With what should be achieved.

Their trainers told them they'd no worth
Beyond what they're assigned.
And this would be the destiny
By which they'd be defined.

They tried indoctrinating them
To act as though a drone
But how successful they had been
Was still a great unknown.

Dissension with the Project

Pete thought the project had been wrong
In concept and design.
These girls had not been volunteers
Who'd signed the dotted line.

They ripped them from their families
Within the dead of night
Their parents had been terrified
When faced with all that might.

They all were taken from their homes
And forced to play Blank's games.
Where they had shown them no respect
Nor ever learned their names.

Though now he was a part of it,
It had not been his choice.
For he simply had his orders
Which left him with no voice.

He thought the plan a gross mistake
But who was he to tell?
He chose to serve his country, but
This project born of hell.

The One Who Pulled the Strings

When Skye had seen Blank on the phone
Blank's secret was revealed.
There'd been someone who pulled the strings
Which was a fact concealed.

Whomever had been on the phone
Of him she was afraid.
Skye noticed how in her response
Few comments had been made.

It was clear she got directives,
Though free to improvise.
For the results that were desired
She would not compromise.

When guards noticed Skye was watching,
They hurried Skye away.
Though they had been oblivious
To what Blank had to say.

Although Skye was disappointed
That she had gained no clue
To what was the identity
Of he who Blank spoke to.

The Reports

The Major was beside himself
With reports he received.
These girls were not the innocents
He was led to believe.

Though his men were battle tested
Who were strangers to fear.
These girls, it seemed, had freaked them out
Whenever they came near.

For Chris had seemed a natural
To master hand-to-hand.
She had innate abilities
They could not understand.

Her whole body was a weapon
For which they'd no defense.
Where trainers found they were helpless
When Chris went on offense.

Jade's muscular development
Had seemed to be surreal.
Although she had been feminine
Her strength was very real.

For they found that Jade was stronger
Than anyone on staff.
Which had made the trainers wary
Of mocking her or laugh.

No guard had wished to be assigned
An escort to watch Skye.
For all of them had been freaked out
They could not to her lie.

She always knew their ev'ry thought
And sometimes could predict
What could spark a disagreement
That led to a conflict.

These girls had been more dangerous
Than what he had been told.
And he blamed Doctor Blank for it
Who he had wished to scold.

Under Constant Scrutiny

Blank's monitors were ev'rywhere
As she on them kept tab.
She did not trust in happenstance
But Intel wished to grab.

She'd no need for conspiracy
Where she's in line of fire.
If they knew they were monitored
They'd dare not to conspire.

The guards had, too, been monitored
As they Blank did not trust.
So, she had kept a watchful eye
Because she thought she must.

Now under constant scrutiny
There was no place to hide.
There were no secrets to be kept
That Blank could not have eyed.

The girls had felt they were exposed
With lack of privacy.
They felt that anything they did
Blank was able to see.

But in time the squad discovered
Where all the blind spots were.
Though Blank had been oblivious
That they were on to her.

For Kat had spotted ev'ryone
Where none escaped her sight.
Though still they had been monitored
They knew where was the site.

The Night They Came Together

Jill saw the fear that they had felt
And knew what she must do.
So, she called them all together
To tell them what she knew.

They felt at some point someone knew
That justice was not served.
This fate which had been sprung on them
Was truly undeserved.

But they'd no one but each other
On whom they could rely.
Though Pete a possibility
As he had caught Jade's eye.

They'd have to make the best of things
While they were still alive.
For now, there only was one goal
And that was to survive.

Jill told the others to comply
With what they would be taught.
Some day from it they'd benefit.
For now, it's time they bought.

And that night they came together
As each had seen the need.
Now none of them would be alone.
On that they all agreed.

The One in Charge

Major Miller told Doctor Blank
He'd not appreciate
The facts she tried to hide from him
As though she could dictate.

But Blank told him it's her project
Where he was to assist.
So, his bitching and complaining
He needed to desist.

Blank said she was the one in charge
Which he should not forget.
She'd tell him what she thought he'd need
To stave off any threat.

The Major had been furious
But found his hands were tied.
For Blank had been the one in charge
Though logic it defied.

The guards had never cared for her
Believing she was cruel.
She had shown she was sadistic
And anger quick to fuel.

He thought, perhaps, he'd been assigned
Because they were not sure
If Doctor Blank's true intentions
Had really been that pure.

Blank's use of Motivation

Blank thought fear was motivation
But when that fear was lost
She knew that she would lose control
Where revenge they'd exhaust.

The collars, thus, had been a must
To hold the upper hand.
She thought pain was the incentive
To make them understand

They had no say in what occurred
With training her domain.
Where any choice to not comply
Would then result in pain.

The remote was Blank's companion
She had no fear to use.
Where anything that annoyed her
Or order they'd refuse.

Jill was the beneficiary
Who took the most abuse.
For Blank abhorred her attitude
Or used that as excuse.

Their Lawyer's Confession

Jill's parents had made overtures
To contact all the rest.
Those whose daughters had been taken
But protests were suppressed.

Their parents had not given up
But pathway was unclear.
The higher in the courts they went
The more had grown their fear.

No judge, it seemed, would intercede
As though some threat was made.
Or those who'd been responsible
Caused them to be afraid.

Then their lawyers had confided
Something else was in play
Beyond what were legalities
The courts had turned away.

Their daughters had been targeted
Though why, they could not say.
But it seemed like the government
Was involved in some way.

They said the matter they'd pursue
But there's no guarantee
Their daughters they would see again
Or know where they may be.

The Incident

One evening to the Dorm returned
To gain a brief respite
When Kat noticed Lynn was absent
Which she had thought not right.

Kat beat upon the Dorm room door
To question where Lynn went.
Where Peter was the one on guard
Who said to clinic sent.

It seemed her training took a turn
Trainers did not expect.
Where Lynn had suffered injuries
When defense she'd neglect.

Doctor Reed had been horrified
When first he had seen Lynn.
He doubted that she could survive
With the shape she was in.

Pete called some guards to take his place
And then he grabbed Kat's hand.
They raced through the facility
Despite it had been banned.

When at last they reached the clinic
Peter led Kat inside.
Where they found Lynn was unconscious
As Kat broke down and cried.

Lynn had taken quite a beating
With injuries severe.
Kat asked the doctor what occurred
Though answer was unclear.

Trainers called it an accident
But Kat had not been sure.
To her it seemed there was intent
But evidence obscure.

When they returned Kat then told Jill
The facts that she had known.
Though there were unanswered questions
On which no light was shone.

A Lack of Reason

There was no reason Lynn should die
For Blank to make a point.
But if it's war that Blank desired
They would not disappoint.

Blank seemed to be a petty bitch
Who always got her way.
And seemed a tantrum she would throw
If any should say nay.

The girls had thought Blank crossed the line
With what occurred to Lynn.
This truly had been undeserved
And never should have been.

They thought respect they had been due
As they'd cooperate.
But Blank, it seemed, incapable
Of anything but hate.

Confrontation and Defiance

Jill beat upon the Dorm room door
Until response was gained.
She wanted to see Doctor Blank
With anger unrestrained.

When Jill confronted Doctor Blank
She had been really mad.
Jill said they're done with secrecy
And Blank had proved a cad.

Where was the justice they were due
And why were they confined?
What purpose were they meant to serve
Which still was undefined?

They'd come into their homes at night
To spirit them away.
There had been protests that were lodged
But parents had no say.

And what about their families
Who they were forced to leave?
Were any options left to them
Besides the need to grieve?

The trainers under Doctor Blank
Were whom Jill dared accuse.
Jill was sick of brutal treatment
And Lynn dared to abuse.

Jill said that they were done with it
Which angered Doctor Blank.
Who then quickly grabbed the remote
As to her knees Jill sank.

Jill suffered in pure agony
Till consciousness was lost.
But never asked for Blank to stop
In fear what that may cost.

Then Blank sneered, "For her defiance
A penalty was due."
Then had the guards drag Jill away
As with her Blank was through.

The Project Placed in Jepoardy

It seemed that Blank had been disturbed
With what the guards had done.
Disregarding her directive
And restraint showing none,

The project placed in jeopardy
As rage they'd not restrained.
The girl, she heard, was critical
Though Reed said hope remained.

Blank said there was no going back
In light of what they'd done.
The girls would be more difficult
As rules may chose to shun.

She'd placed her faith and trust in them
But found it commandeered.
Those four Blank held responsible
Then simply disappeared.

She'd told the trainers from the start
And made it very clear
Failure would spawn repercussions
That would be most severe.

The Major's Thoughts on Doctor Blank

It's true she's a sadistic bitch
For whom he never cared.
She'd flaunted her authority
In ways he never dared.

Her project he thought asinine
And way over the top.
But with the funding she received
He knew she'd never stop.

These girls, he thought, were victims, too,
That Blank had dared enslave.
She stole them from their families
So, project she could save.

He thought her backers were suspect
In motive and desire.
And wondered if the girls' futures
Were what they would aspire.

For Blank had given them no choice
But do as she would say.
She had not cared a whit for them
And lives would throw away.

The Discerning of Their Purpose

When the rest returned from training
They found Jill on the floor.
She'd barely regained consciousness
Which they could not ignore.

Chris lifted Jill's head to her lap
And gently stroked her hair.
Then as Jill's mind began to clear
Where she grew more aware.

Brie then asked Jill what had happened,
When Skye had calmly said
With Jill's clear act of defiance
That Blank had wished Jill dead.

In shock all eyes had turned to Skye,
Who said it was a gift.
She had a sense for certain things
That sometimes was makeshift.

Jill said that's why they'd been chosen
With each of them unique.
Then Skye remarked in layman's terms,
Blank thought them each a freak.

But to what end were they captured
Kat had dared to inquire.
Jill said that Skye could answer that
Then watched seconds expire.

To Skye it had been obvious
With training they'd received.
They were to be the hand of God
To serve as Blank believed.

They're meant to be a black ops squad
To Jill that had been clear.
They'd strip them of humanity
And all that they held dear.

Lynn's Secret

When Lynn, at last, returned to them
She would not speak of it.
Nor what had sparked the incident
That left her less than fit.

Although Skye could not explain it
She saw in her mind's eye
What Lynn refused to speak about
And reasons she knew why.

She'd reached out to give Lynn a hug
Though found that with the touch
Lynn's thoughts had been revealed to he
As soon as they would clutch.

Their trainers had seen Lynn kiss Kat
Where Lynn was next in line.
Blank's orders had been crystal clear
Where love they must decline.

For love would only make them weak
And serve to cloud their mind.
Love would make them vulnerable
With choices hard to find.

But though love had been forbidden
It could not be denied.
Yet, their trainers had their orders.
Rules were to be applied.

Though Lynn had staged a strong defense,
It had been four on one.
Yet, when the lesson was complete
Lynn had been more than done.

The medics had been quickly called
But when they had arrived,
Found injuries were serious
And lucky she survived.

Then when Blank had heard the story
She nearly lost her mind.
For these girls were very special
And difficult to find.

Next Blank pronounced their punishment
Which had been quite severe.
Where all four trainers were dismissed
Or made to disappear.

It had only been a second
When Skye had stepped away.
Convinced Lynn's secrets where her own
And nothing would Skye say.

The Detriment

Chris feared she lived on borrowed time
As destiny was set.
They held her life within their hands
If their goals were not met.

She claimed that she'd been put upon
As this she'd not deserved.
As though the others volunteered
And had the project served.

The anger that had welled in Brie
Made her wish to lash out.
And maybe beat Chris half to death
To suffocate her pout.

For Brie found Chris a whinny bitch
Who constantly complained.
She'd not faced the situation
That to her was explained.

They all were placed in the same boat
Where the rest tried to deal.
But Chris tried to convince herself
That none of it was real.

Her presence was a detriment
That put them all on edge.
She'd shown them a poor attitude
As though she walked the ledge.

While Chris wallowed in self-pity
The facts she had ignored.
Their situation serious
With training they abhorred.

Brie demanded that Chris grow up
And not act like a child.
She had to come to grips with it
And stop acting beguiled.

Jade's Disappearances

Peter would sometimes come for Jade
And escort her away.
Wherever Pete had taken her
Jade had refused to say.

As though it all was prearranged
But only known to them.
For Jade would never hesitate
When she went off with him.

Some feared that he took liberties
And she had been naïve.
But when they had confronted her
Denied what they'd perceive.

They weren't allowed to have free run
Of the facility.
So, it had been quite difficult
To find some privacy.

Jade said with all the monitors
Alone time had been hard.
But Peter knew a special place
Where they're not under guard.

Where they would simply talk and dream
Of what was yet to come.
And even reminisce a bit
About where they were from.

As Training had Intensified

The more rigid grew their training
The more they would resist.
With their trainers unforgiving
And prone to use a fist

While beatings weren't unusual
They were somewhat controlled.
Blank had ordered that no scarring
Was allowed to be doled.

The remote was the providence
Reserved for Doctor Blank.
The trainers were more physical
As lower they had sank.

Resentment grew each day they trained
Where hate was all they knew.
As no compassion had been shown
As Blank thought none was due.

Questions

In a moment of privacy
That Pete and Jade had shared.
She'd not wished to spoil that moment
But questions she had dared.

Jade looked at Pete with pleading eyes
And asked if it was true
The world had now abandoned them
And parents had no clue.

Pete said he's not completely sure
If all of that was true.
He knew that they were prisoners
With little he could do.

But he told her he'd no knowledge
Of what her parents knew.
For he, like her, was quarantined
And had no outside view.

The only thing he knew for sure
That she he would protect.
Because she'd clearly claimed his heart
Though prayed none could detect.

The Awakening

When Chris discovered Brie was right,
She truly felt ashamed.
The others not responsible
And, thus, could not be blamed.

Their circumstance had been the same
As that which Chris had faced.
For none of them had asked for this,,
Thus, her anger misplaced.

Those older showed an inner strength
That she did not possess.
But she refused to turn to them
With weakness to profess.

They showed a class of character
That she'd not, yet, acquired.
She looked to them for leadership
As to what was required.

Whatever course they chose to take
Would be the course she'd choose.
And she would face the penalties
With nothing more to lose.

She wanted to give proof to them
That she, too, could be strong.
For in the end, what mattered most,
Was show that she'd belong.

The Weapons They Created

Their training grew to integrate
Them into groups and pairs.
With teamwork a necessity
To catch foes unawares.

Their trainers also multiplied
For few won one-on-one.
In fact, the girls were so adept
It's rare a trainer won.

While their mastery of weapons
Had seemed to be surreal.
Though each possessed a favorite
That had its own appeal.

Though as their training had progressed
Their trainers came to fear
That these girls had now been weapons
Who had been without peer.

The Jackal

The Jackal was the specialist
The other trainers feared.
For he was a true mechanic
Who death had engineered.

The Jackal was anonymous
And could be anyone.
He had been a trained assassin
That Blank had doted on.

His face was covered by a mask
To hide identity.
His specialty had been to kill
And kills, he claimed, plenty.

He was a master of black ops
Who left no clues behind.
His targets he'd eliminate
Then wipe them from his mind.

The Jackal was the very best
The government had trained.
No mission was too difficult
Nor fear had entertained.

Major Miller was unhappy
The Jackal was brought in.
For the Jackal's reputation
Was to death he's akin.

Caught up in a Nightmare

Legalities and civil rights
Had no place in their world.
They were caught up in a nightmare
Into which they were hurled.

They're subject to brutalities
That had been undeserved.
For none of them had volunteered
This mission to have served.

And instructors had forgotten
They still were teenagers.
They had not been prepared for this.
As to this they're strangers.

They'd not been raised from birth in camps
Where they'd been trained to kill.
And they had a sense of values
Parents worked to instill.

So, there was no quarter given
Nor no compassion shown.
For Blank wanted each girl broken
So, what's reborn she'd own.

Trainers versus the Guards

Skye had sensed that there were tensions
Between trainers and guards.
The groups seemed polar opposites
With each shown no regards.

The guards had shown them dignity
While trainers had no clue.
The guards had shown them some respect
While trainers thought none due.

The guards were mostly courteous.
To trainers they were dirt.
The trainers inconsiderate
If they're injured or hurt.

While the guards had been protective,
Their trainers had not cared.
The guards, they found, looked out for them.
Their trainers had not dared.

Skye knew it would not take that much
To set the two at odds.
Which should be a new specialty
As member of death squads.

For Blank had kept a watchful eye
On all that had occurred.
And cared less about their comfort
Nor what they had endured.

Confrontation with the Jackal

The Jackal bragged that he had known
A thousand ways to kill.
That he had seemed so passionate
Left the girls feeling chilled.

The Jackal grabbed Kat by the throat
And to it placed a blade.
It all had happened in a flash
Where Kat had no sound made.

But the Jackal had seemed smitten
When Brie turned on the charm.
When it seemed he was distracted
And easy to disarm.

Though the Jackal had a weakness
With moral compass flawed.
He had no sense of right and wrong
And could not be declawed.

He claimed whatever he wanted
And he had wanted Brie.
But she'd refused his advances
Which had made him angry.

He started to get physical
Which caught Brie by surprise.
So, Chris had come to Brie's defense
Though actions she'd despise.

Though the Jackal was a killer,
He killed through pure deceit.
As a master of subterfuge
Where death was his to mete.

But if his victim was aware
And able to fight back
The Jackal had been limited
In scope of his attack.

Then when the Jackal had faced Chris
Jill jumped him from behind.
The Jackal was no match for both
Though exit could not find.

He was a victim of his pride
And meant to do them harm.
When Chris had caught him in a grip
And deftly broke his arm.

The other trainers sneered at him
Believing he deserved
The beating that was given him
They wished they had observed.

Then the Jackal had been recalled
In fear of what he'd do.
The government would not admit
The girls had scared it, too.

Their Final Exercise

It was their final exercise
That Blank, herself, designed.
And the Major was the target
That the girls were assigned.

Their objective to capture him
But he's not to be harmed.
The guards had not been notified
Thus, they would be well armed.

Because the guards were not informed
That this had been a test.
That way the girls would face the guards
When guards were at their best.

The trainers would evaluate
Their level of success.
While Blank the final arbiter
In their use of finesse.

He had layers of protection
They'd have to penetrate.
Where stealth would be of the essence
If they're to graduate.

There were guards outside his office
And both ends of the hall.
A stairway had led up to it
Where two guards had stood tall.

There had been no outside access
As it claimed the sixth floor.
Its walls had been steel reinforced
As was his office door.

It's Jill who had developed it,
The plan they'd execute.
Who warned the timing critical
And had to follow suit.

From the rooftop Chris had accessed
The ventilator shaft.
Though she was a contortionist
Skye still had thought her daft.

Then Brie approached the stairway guards
Unleashing all her charms.
Which allowed the rest to sneak upstairs
While raising no alarms.

Next Lynn had cast an illusion
That hid Jade, Skye and Kat.
Before the guards had known they're there
That was the end of that.

Chris then dropped from a ceiling vent
While Jade had breached the door.
Before the Major could respond
He was knocked to the floor.

Chris threw a hood over his head
While Lynn the window broke.
And with the Major tightly bound
They lowered the angry bloke.

Jill waited on the ground for him
To ensure he wasn't harmed.
While Blank had said she was impressed
In how guards were disarmed.

The Major had been furious
That Blank made him a pawn.
If this was to embarrass him
It's too far she had gone.

Graduation

They were about to graduate
With training near complete.
Though with one final exercise
In which they must compete.

The dangers that awaited them
To Blank of no concern.
She thought them all expendable
If none of them return.

Although the trainers they despised,
They had no wish to kill.
Blank said it was their only choice
As trainers surely will.

The trainers were caught by surprise
As they had been betrayed.
For Blank had played them all as fools
With how their trust repaid.

As the girls had faced their trainers
They recognized the fear.
For that the girls experienced
When first they were brought here.

But now both trained and confident
There was no longer fear.
There was only self-assurance
Their skills were without peer.

Though the trainers begged for mercy
The girls' hands had been tied.
Where they were left without a choice
And at the end had cried.

Their Evaluation

Though Blank impressed how they performed
Her praise she had withheld.
She was distraught they felt remorse
And wished them more hard-shelled.

Blank only cared about results
And not their comfort zone.
They were meant to be assassins
With guilt to never own.

So, in some ways she felt she failed
As she could clearly see
She'd no success in stripping them
Of their humanity.

But they still had been efficient
As trainers they dispatched.
But they lacked the killer instinct
On which she'd wished they'd latched.

The Moment of Epiphany

Who knows what people may decide
When life is on the line?
What depth to which they'd dare to sink
If to death won't resign?

The moment of epiphany
When some choice must be made.
To either struggle to survive
Or into death just fade.

For most, the choice is obvious
Because a primal drive.
As we will do most anything
In order to survive.

The problem that was posed to them,
To either fight or die
Had been ruled by primal instinct
In how they gave reply.

But now remorse would eat at them
As with guilt overcome.
For now the fact they had survived
Was what they suffered from.

That moment of epiphany
They came to understand
The will to live that they possessed
Was what guided their hand.

Miller's Request

The Major wanted Blank removed
And threatened to resign.
For she had been responsible
In concept and design.

Her project was a travesty
In what the girls had faced.
She was sadistic in approach
And, in his mind, disgraced.

She showed no hint of empathy
For what she put them through.
And criticized their ev'ry move
As though her favor due.

She allowed no amenities
Unless they had been earned.
But never seemed to be impressed
With how much they had learned.

She treated them like prisoners
Though guilty of no crime.
And she showed them no compassion
As she'd not had the time.

But his request had been denied
By those who had believed
Blank's project may be integral
To what could be achieved.

Decision Time

That very night after dinner
The girls agreed to meet.
They filed into the shower room
Where they could be discrete.

The room devoid of monitors
At least, Kat could detect.
So, they felt that they could speak freely
And circumstance dissect.

Jill then said she was not happy
With who she had become.
For Blank had made them murderers
And guilt can't overcome.

When, suddenly, Kat had motioned
For silence in the room.
She heard someone was at the door
Which could well spell their doom.

Skye ventured out to check the door
When she had sensed it's Pete.
And as the door revealed who's there
Jade ran to him to greet.

Jill quickly brought Pete up to speed
With all of their concerns.
They did not like what they'd become
Nor with what they had learned.

They found they all were in agreement
This farce must have an end.
Jill looked around the room and saw
Sisters who're more than friend.

They all agreed they'd rather die
Than buckle to Blank's will.
Before Blank tried to brainwash them
Or even try to kill.

For after what they'd done this day
Who knew what she'd request.
She treated them as though her slaves
To act at her behest.

A bond built through adversity
Had bound them for all time.
Where even if that time was short
Its quality was prime.

They must choose a course of action
Before one's given them.
By then they'd find it was too late
For this life to condemn.

While Pete and Jade held each other
And Kat and Lynn held hands,
Jill knew what she'd propose to them
May have some high demands.

Peter said he would stand with them
Whatever they'd decide.
He'd face the fate that's meant for him
If Jade was by his side.

With Fading Hope

Their parents had not given up
But took a diff'rent route.
They appealed to authorities
To take up their pursuit.

For their daughters had been taken
Within the dead of night
By those who're unidentified
And had not seemed contrite.

The court system had been no help
As all it did was stall.
No judge would even hear them out
As they'd no clues at all.

Investigations were past due
Which should be underway.
For their daughters were still missing
And where, no one could say.

Their parents had not given up
But hope was fading fast.
It seemed that justice was so slow
That evil could outlast.

The Great Escape

Their training nearly was complete
When Blank laid down the law.
They all were to be sterilized
Which was the final straw.

Then Jill told Kat this would not stand
As she was tired of it.
They were no more than guinea pigs
Blank used as she saw fit.

While Lynn deceived the monitors
Their collars Jade removed.
Which released them from Blank's service
And morale had improved.

Jill had known what may await them
But Skye stood by her side.
Where Doctor Blank had been surprised
They'd lost the will to hide.

Next morning when guards came for them
They had refused to go.
Their training, now, had been complete
With nothing more to know.

Jill told the guards that they were done
And refused to comply.
Unless Blank would agree to meet
Till then, she said, goodbye.

When the guard slapped Jill in the face
Jade quickly made him pay.
Jade threw the guard across the room
Where by the wall he'd lay.

Jill cried the moment was at hand
For freedom to reclaim.
They're not the girls who first arrived
Who were docile and tame.

Jill wished their exit more controlled
But Jade had forced their hand.
As other guards would soon approach
For which Jill had not planned.

For now they were the Mantis Squad
Who had been highly trained.
And freedom was their one desire
That could not be restrained.

Then as they streamed into the hall
Pete had awaited them.
It seemed the choice that Peter made
Was keep Jade close to him.

It's gunfire Jill wished to avoid
As they'd no wish to kill.
That road by force was travelled once
Where they'd received their fill.

The guards were not that cognizant
How highly they'd been trained.
So, when the girls were forced to strike
T'was shock they entertained.

The guards were ineffectual
In halting their advance.
For in close quarters, hand-to-hand,
The guards stood little chance.

Then Jill told Skye to take the lead
And she'd catch up somehow.
For there's a detour Jill must take
To satisfy a vow.

Blank was hiding in her office
When Jill burst through the door.
Blank had begged Jill not to kill her
Though not what Jill came for.

Jill revealed to Blank a secret
Blank had not wished to hear.
For Blank had made some enemies
Which Blank should greatly fear.

Jill made Blank put on a collar
As Jill grabbed the remote.
Jill smiled as she pushed the button
While Blank grabbed at her throat.

Jill had wondered what the range was
As she slipped out the door.
She could have left remote behind
But wished to up the score.

Jill had met little resistance
When others she rejoined.
It seemed a path was cleared for them
As none in conflict joined.

The Major told his guards stand down
For they were overmatched.
The trainers did their job too well
Based on those they'd dispatched.

He'd no hope of containing them
Though lives wished to preserve.
He'd no desire in stopping them
As freedom they'd deserve.

When they saw the gate before them
Peter assumed the lead.
When next a random shot rang out
Where Pete began to bleed.

Jade ran to him as he collapsed
And tried to stop the flow.
But there was nothing she could do
Except to let him go.

Without a comment Chris and Lynn
Had gone to comfort Jade.
Then gently pulled her to her feet
Away from where Pete laid.

The Refusal

While Jade had refused to leave him,
There's nothing she could do.
Pete's body just a lifeless husk
That Jade had clung onto.

Skye had tried to coax her away
But Jade refused to leave.
She'd rather stay and die with him
Than for him live and grieve.

Emotions had a grip on her
Where she had not thought straight.
So, when the others pulled her off
Her heart was filled with hate.

Pete had only shown her kindness
And for that he had died.
Jade found the pain was so intense
She had not even cried.

With Freedom Gained

Jill looked into the Major's eyes
And saw that it was done.
Too many lives already lost.
Let Pete be the last one.

And when the gates were opened wide
All seven had walked free.
A problem for the government
That it did not foresee.

They'd walked away and not looked back
With remote tossed aside.
Jill wondered what the range had been
But hoped that Blank had fried.

For now, that they were fully trained
It's justice that they sought.
Where some part of the government
Had just some vengeance bought.

A Sigh of Relief

The Major sighed in great relief
None of his guards were killed.
There'd been extensive injuries
Which left him a bit chilled.

What exactly did Blank create
That fought like a machine?
The girls had looked so innocent
But when provoked turned mean.

They fought with such efficiency
It almost was surreal.
His Men were grizzled veterans
Though with them could not deal.

Now that the girls had been set free
He wondered what came next.
Would they fade into the sunset
Or government perplex?

In Light of what Occurred

In light of what had just occurred
He ordered Blank be found.
He wanted her in custody
And then restrained and bound.

They found Blank inside her office
Just twitching on the ground.
She'd been fitted with a collar
But no remote was found.

Though when they removed her collar
No thanks did she provide.
Instead, she reached up to her desk
With evidence to hide.

They took from her what she had grabbed
And drug her to her feet.
They said the Major asked for her
So he, she soon would meet.

The Major saw the heartless bitch
That Blank had now become.
Who thought she was impervious
To charges yet to come.

The Major called the higher ups
To tell them what occurred.
The Mantis Squad had all escaped
And injuries incurred.

He'd insufficient resources
To mount a search for them.
For any that he would dispatch
Would risk both life and limb.

He blamed it all on Doctor Blank
Who pushed the girls too far.
She'd turned them into murderers
Which seemed had left a scar.

He had Blank in his custody
Awaiting their command.
The Major thought she should be tried
And staff made to disband.

Someone must be Accountable

Now that her project was complete
Blank hated what she heard.
The Mantis Squad was still intact
For which she now must gird.

The government had recalled Blank
As it held her to blame.
The Mantis Squad was now a threat
It had no wish to claim.

Someone must be accountable
For the deaths that occurred.
Blank had tried to blame the Major
As guilt she wished transferred.

For Blank had failed to recognize
The power she released.
She thought she had control of it
But found it merely leased.

And now, the piper must be paid
Where Blank would take the fall.
For she had been the one in charge
And author of it all.

Blank's Trial

The government had disavowed
That it gave its consent.
Blank had proceeded on her own
Despite its strong dissent.

Her funding was untraceable
Or so, had been its claim.
But few had truly trusted that
Had been its true endgame.

It said that it would right this wrong
No matter what it took.
But most had given credence that
It just wished off the hook.

The shock was unmistakable
When they had come for her.
She was convinced she would be freed
But that hope she'd defer.

Though to show its sincerity
Blank's trial was very swift.
Where length of sentence she received
It said had been a gift.

Epilog

Blank was placed in solitary
As there had been some threats.
Though they found no confirmation
They wished to hedge their bets.

Then one night there was a blackout
That came as a surprise.
Though when the power was restored
She stared at her demise.

The Mantis Squad had shared her cell
With vengeance in their eyes.
For all that she had put them through
It's death she'd come to prize.

Blank knew that paybacks were a bitch
As Jill gave her a clue.
If they found opportunity
She'd get what she was due.

It's said that Blank had lost her mind
Though no one had known why.
From a blackout she imagined
In which she thought she'd die.